THE COLOR DAY COACH

by Gail Herman
illustrated by Anthony Lewis

Kane Press
New York

For Lizzie, runner, baker, and team player—G.H.
For Isabella, Emilia, and Rory—A.L.

Library of Congress Cataloging-in-Publication Data

Names: Herman, Gail, 1959- author. | Lewis, Anthony, 1966- illustrator.
Title: The Color Day coach / by Gail Herman ; illustrated by Anthony Lewis.
Description: New York : Kane Press, 2018. | Series: Makers make it work |
Summary: When Jake, the best athlete in his class, breaks his leg just before the Color Day contest, he contributes by coaching his teammates and baking them cupcakes. Includes tips about baking.
Identifiers: LCCN 2017027414 (print) | LCCN 2017039393 (ebook) | ISBN 9781575659947 (ebook) | ISBN 9781575659930 (pbk) | ISBN 9781635920130 (reinforced library binding)
Subjects: | CYAC: Teamwork (Sports)—Fiction. | Contests—Fiction. | Coaches (Athletics)—Fiction. | Baking—Fiction. | Schools—Fiction.
Classification: LCC PZ7.H4315 (ebook) | LCC PZ7.H4315 Cls 2018 (print) | DDC [E]—dc23
LC record available at https://lccn.loc.gov/2017027414

10 9 8 7 6 5 4 3 2 1

First published in the United States of America in 2018 by Kane Press, Inc.
Printed in China

Book Design: Michelle Martinez

Makers Make It Work is a trademark of Kane Press, Inc.

Visit us online at **www.kanepress.com**

 Like us on Facebook
facebook.com/kanepress

 Follow us on Twitter
@KanePress

Jake stared out the classroom window. He couldn't wait to be outside.

"I have exciting news," Mr. Adams said. "Color Day is next week."

Yes! Jake loved Color Day! The races! The contests! Everything!

"I hope we are T-O-G-E-T-H-E-R," Cole
told Jake.

Jake grinned. Cole liked to spell words.
Usually, Jake understood what he was saying.

"Everyone wants to be on Jake's team," Ella said. "He's the best athlete in the grade."

Mr. Adams handed out a list of the teams. Jake and Cole high-fived. They were both on the Green Team. So was Ella.

Outside at recess, Jake said, "Let's practice for Color Day!" The fence was the starting line. The big oak tree was the finish.

Jake, Ella, Cole, and a few other kids lined up.

"I'm running to get in S-H-A-P-E," Cole said.

Jake grinned. Cole was the smartest kid in class. But he was just about the slowest, too.

Everyone took off. Jake didn't look at the others.
He knew he was ahead.
Then something awful happened.
He stepped in a hole. His ankle twisted. He fell.

All the kids stopped.

"Are you all right?" Cole asked. He was so worried, he didn't even spell.

"I don't know," said Jake. He felt like crying. His leg really hurt.

"Don't move," said Ella. "Your leg may be broken."

Ella was right. Jake's leg was broken. He came home from the hospital in a cast.

His friends could sign it. And it didn't really hurt anymore. It wouldn't be that bad—except that Color Day was next week!

"Remember, no running," Jake's mom said. "And I mean it."

Jake groaned. He had picked a bright green cast—just for Color Day. But he wished he could race, too. He wanted to help his team win!

The next day, Jake went to school on crutches. Cole and Ella rushed over.

"I love your cast!" said Ella.

"I'm still G-L-A-D you're on our team," Cole added.

They were being nice. Now that Jake was hurt, it didn't matter what team he was on.

He tried to help in other ways. That afternoon, Jake set up a relay for the Green Team.

"Start with your head down," he told Cole. "That helps you go faster."

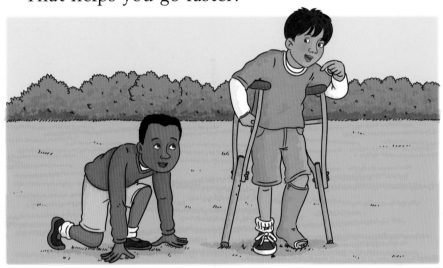

"Don't slow up near the finish!" he said to Ella. "Keep running right through the line."

Jake watched everyone hop and skip and
run. He shouted out tips until he had to leave.
Every day, he coached his friends.

"I wish I could help my team more," Jake told his mom on the day before Color Day.

"Well, you're wearing green." His mom pointed to his cast. "That shows team spirit. And we can buy green spray to color your hair. It washes right out."

Jake nodded. "Let's go!"

At the store, Jake picked up the green hair spray. He tried to smile. But a sigh slipped out instead.

Too bad he couldn't use his hands to help his team win Color Day! They worked fine.

"You know what?" his mom said. "You need a special treat."

Jake's mom led him to the bakery. Cupcakes were lined up all in a row. Chocolate, vanilla, strawberry. Brown, white, red. Just seeing them made him feel better.

Suddenly Jake had an idea—a way to help his team!

"Mom!" he said. "I could bake cupcakes for the team. But they have to be green!"

When they got home, Jake went right to the kitchen. Did he have everything?

Flour? Check.

Eggs? Check.

Frosting and sprinkles? Check.

Milk and butter and the rest? Check!

Attention, bakers! Here's a tip. For better baking, let things like butter, milk, and eggs warm to room temperature before mixing them.

Jake set out two bowls—one for vanilla batter and one for chocolate. Then he measured carefully. First flour, then sugar, butter, and milk. One by one, he added the items from the recipe.

He squirted food coloring into each bowl and mixed everything together. Finally he poured the batter into two cupcake trays. His mom put both trays into the oven.

Now all he had to do was wait!

It's important to measure carefully like Jake did. Use the flat side of a butter knife to level the flour in a measuring cup so it's just right.

Jake waited and waited. Suddenly, he sniffed. Something smelled funny. "Mom!" he cried. "The cupcakes are burning!"

He'd forgotten to set the timer!

Know your measurements!
3 teaspoons = 1 tablespoon
8 tablespoons = ½ cup
2 cups = 1 pint

Jake rushed to the oven. Smoke filled the air. His mom pulled out the trays. His cupcakes weren't green. They were black!

Everything was ruined!

It was so late now. He was tired. Maybe he should just stay home for Color Day.

It helps to be organized! First read through the recipe and prepare everything you need. Turn on the oven right away so it's ready for the batter— and don't forget the timer!

To measure liquids, use a clear measuring cup with lines and a spout.

Then Jake took a deep breath. He still wanted to help his team. So what if he was tired? He'd been tired before, playing sports and running races. And he hadn't quit then.

He'd just have to start over.

Once again, Jake poured and mixed, and mixed some more. His arm was getting tired, but he kept going. And this time, the cupcakes came out fine! The vanilla ones were light green. The chocolate ones were dark green.

Jake added blue and yellow food coloring to vanilla frosting. When the cupcakes cooled, he spread the green frosting.

Food Coloring Math!
yellow + blue = green
blue + red = purple
red + yellow = orange

Not all the cupcakes were perfect. One looked really lopsided. Jake decided that would be his. He used sprinkles to write a "J" on it.

Then he made a "C" for Cole on a vanilla cupcake, and an "E" for Ella on a chocolate one. He made cool shapes on the rest.

The next day, Jake and his mom drove to the school field. Jake saw a rainbow of colors, and kids everywhere. Some kids were stretching. Some were running in place. Everyone was getting ready—except for the Green Team.

His team sat under a tree. They all looked unhappy.

Then Cole saw Jake.

"Jake is here to C-H-E-E-R!" he shouted.

"I have a special treat, too!" Jake told them. "Cupcakes! I made them myself."

"They look yummy!" Ella reached for one.

Cole said, "Let's save them for later. After we W-I-N!"

Now the Green Team was ready to race!
They stretched. They ran in place.

Jake grinned. He was helping his team—
broken leg and all.

Tweet! The principal blew her whistle.
The races were about to begin!

Cole was slow and steady in the egg and spoon race.

Ella raced through the pizza delivery relay.

Everyone pulled together for the tug-of-war.

Jake even tried the beanbag toss. He didn't
need two good legs for that!

In the end, Red won. Still, Jake's team had come close.

"Green Team is T-E-R-R-I-F-I-C!" shouted Cole.

"And so are these cupcakes!" Ella said.

Jake smiled at his friends. Now he knew—when you have a broken leg, use your head and your hands instead.

And just like that, he had another idea. Next week was the school spelling bee. . . .

Learn Like a Maker

Jake's broken leg meant he couldn't join in the Color Day races, but that didn't stop him from helping his team. He found a different way—by making cupcakes!

Look Back

- ❌ On page 18, it says to measure carefully. Why do you think this is an important skill?

- ❌ Look at pages 20–22. What went wrong with Jake's first batch of cupcakes? What does it show you about Jake's character that he tried again even though he was tired?

Try This!

Cupcake Lab

Find a recipe for cupcakes. Try to think of a way to change it by adding or substituting an ingredient. Sardines would taste awful with chocolate, but what might taste yummy? If you're substituting ingredients be sure to think about the type of ingredient you are using. For example, you wouldn't substitute lemonade for flour because one is liquid and the other is dry. With an adult on hand, mix up your new recipe and bake the cupcakes.

Invite friends to taste your new cupcake. Record who gives the recipe a "Thumbs-up" and who says, "Try Again."

Did your cupcakes taste good? What would you try next time?